A Medal
for Murphy

A Medal for Murphy

Written by
MELISSA FORNEY

Illustrated by
JAMES RICE

PELICAN PUBLISHING COMPANY
GRETNA 1987

First printing, March 1987
First paperback printing, September 2000

Library of Congress Cataloging-in-Publication Data

Odom, Melissa W.
    A medal for Murphy.

    Summary: Murphy, a stray dog living in the streets of a
small town, proves to the townspeople that he is a hero and
not a dangerous menace.
    [1. Dogs—Fiction] I. Rice, James, 1934-   , ill. II. Title.
PZ7.02383Me 1987   [Fic]   86-25369
ISBN 1-56554-832-9 (pbk.)

Printed in Hong Kong
Published by Pelican Publishing Company, Inc.
1000 Burmaster Street, Gretna, Louisiana 70053

Murphy the Mutt was nobody's dog. In fact, he was the town pest. He didn't have a name back then, and no one in Taylorsville even knew where he came from. But he seemed to like the little town.

Soft yellow lights twinkled through the curtains of friendly kitchens. Murphy could see mothers stirring oatmeal. He could hear the sizzle of eggs frying and the pop-pop of bacon cooking. He stretched his long, lean body and set out to find some breakfast. By the time the shopkeepers were unlocking their stores and sweeping off their porches, he had already found some cold scrambled eggs in Mrs. Hazlitt's garbage can.

Murphy was glad that little Aaron wasn't too fond of scrambled eggs, because that meant he could always count on a few leftovers. He really didn't mean to tip the garbage can over, but the piece of bacon down in the bottom smelled too good to resist. Licking his whiskers, he skipped off down the alley to Johnson's Barber Shop.

Old Mr. Johnson, who couldn't see very well, was sipping some coffee and squinting at his morning paper. There on the saucer with his coffee was a fat, sugary doughnut. Unseen by Mr. Johnson, Murphy sat down and waited. When Mr. Johnson licked his finger and turned the pages of his newspaper, Murphy saw his chance. He stretched out his neck and gobbled the doughnut down in one swift bite.

"Why, you lousy mutt!" roared Mr. Johnson as Murphy dodged and scooted down the steps of the barber shop. "It's getting so a body can't trust *anyone* anymore!" Murphy just scampered off to search for more tidbits.

By mid-morning his belly bulged with a satisfying meal of chicken scraps, several English peas from a TV dinner, a saucer of milk that belonged to Mrs. Whitmore's kitty, and a stale tuna sandwich.

Tired from his morning's exercise, Murphy looked for a quiet place where he could nap. Just before he stretched out on the burlap sacks behind Sneed's Grocery Store, he saw something that made his mouth water.

Ludgie Brown, Mr. Sneed's vegetable man, was taking a long drink from a frosty glass mug. "Mm, mm, *mmm!*" exclaimed Ludgie. "That root beer sure tastes good on a hot day. I'll save the rest for when I'm finished unloading all these vegetables." He turned back to his work, setting the mug on a crate next to the burlap sacks.

Murphy's wet, black nose sniffed the delicious root beer. His tail wagged fast. What luscious, thick brown foam there was on top of the drink in the mug! When Ludgie's back was turned, Murphy lapped up the foam with a quick slurp. Foam covered his nose and made his tail wag even faster. He snorted and lapped at the fizzy root beer.

"Hey!" screamed Ludgie, who had turned around just in time to catch Murphy. "My root beer! Wait till I get my hands on you, mutt!"

Murphy dashed around the corner just as a large head of shriveled lettuce whizzed past him. Ludgie was one mad vegetable man. He ran after the furry brown thief, screaming, "I'm so MAD! Get that DOG! Stop that DOG!"

Murphy, eyes rolling and feet thundering, raced around the front of Sneed's Grocery Store to escape. Mrs. Peabody was sitting on the bench in front of the store. She looked up to see Murphy running away, with the raging Ludgie right behind, hollering, "That DOG makes me so MAD!" She saw the root beer foam on Murphy's face and heard only part of what Ludgie was yelling. *Foam. Mad. Dog.* Those words could only mean one thing. She scrambled to her feet as fast as she could and shrieked, "MAD DOG! RABIES! That dog has rabies!" All of the shoppers in the grocery store rushed out to see what was going on.

"I'm sure you're mistaken, Mrs. Peabody," said Mr. Sneed, the grocer. But all anyone could hear was Mrs. Peabody shrieking, "Mad dog! Somebody had better help Ludgie Brown catch him before he bites somebody!" With that, Mr. Sneed and all the shoppers dropped their groceries and joined in the race to capture Murphy.

As they hurry-scurried down Main Street, old Mr. Johnson called, "What's the rush? Doesn't anyone need a haircut?"

"Didn't you see?" gasped Mr. Sneed. "A vicious, mad dog is on the loose. He's bitten somebody."

"Why, I bet it's the varmint that stole my doughnut this morning!" exclaimed Mr. Johnson. "I could have been attacked—killed!" And laying down his clippers, old Mr. Johnson took off running, faster than anyone had seen him run in a long time.

The crowd turned down Beacon Boulevard and hurried past the office of the town's newspaper, the *Taylorsville Chit-Chat.* Clem Loggins, the editor, had his chair propped back in the doorway and was lighting his pipe. "What's the news? Anybody got any news?" he called when he saw the people approaching.

"A dog with rabies attacked old Mr. Johnson this morning and he's headed toward the park where the children play. We're trying to stop him before he attacks somebody's baby!" called one of the shoppers over her shoulder.

Clem Loggins's pipe fell right out of his mouth. Quick as lightning he yelled, "Get the presses rolling! A mad dog just attacked somebody's baby! Whose baby? I don't know, but I'm going to find out right now. I always get the facts straight." Grabbing his cap, his camera, and a pad and pencil, Clem dashed off to join the ever-growing group.

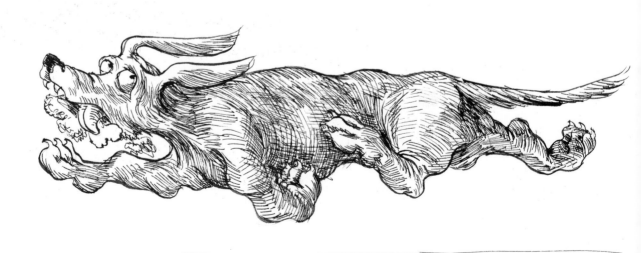

Huffing and puffing down the street, he passed right in front of the police station. "Sheriff Forbus!" shouted the frantic Clem. "You'd better get your gun and your deputies and come with me. There's a mad dog on the loose that's already attacked two people. He's headed for the park. Hurry!"

"Attention all cars, attention all cars!" barked Sheriff Forbus into his police radio. "Mad dog of unknown description headed for the park. Shoot to kill. I repeat, *shoot to kill!*" He pulled his gun out of the bottom drawer of his desk and headed after Clem and the others.

By this time, Murphy was way ahead of Sheriff Forbus and Clem Loggins. He was way ahead of the group of shoppers and old Mr. Johnson. He was even ahead of Ludgie Brown. In fact, he had forgotten all about Ludgie Brown. He was so tired that all he wanted to do was cool off in the pond in the center of the park where all the children played. The water would feel good after all his adventures.

Murphy was not the only one who was interested in the pond. Chubby Rebecca was running on her fat little legs toward the cool, deep water. She was hot from playing in the park, and the water looked like it would be fun to splash in. She toddled out on the dock that the older boys fished from. Her mother was laughing and talking with some other mothers and didn't notice.

When Murphy saw the small girl walking close to the edge of the dock, he sensed danger. Murphy barked to warn Rebecca's mother, but the other children were playing a noisy game of tag, so she couldn't hear him. He walked out onto the dock toward the baby girl.

At that very moment the entire angry mob of Ludgie
Brown, Mr. Sneed, the shoppers, old Mr. Johnson, Clem
Loggins, Sheriff Forbus, and the deputies rushed into the
park looking for the mad dog.

On the dock Rebecca's mother spotted Murphy and the little girl. "My baby!" she shrieked. "Someone stop her! My baby is crawling off the end of the dock! She'll drown!" Rebecca's mother started running toward the dock. Everyone in the park turned to see Rebecca perched on the end of the dock—with Murphy pulling on her diaper with his teeth.

"There he is, men. There's the mad dog," barked Sheriff Forbus into his megaphone. He's attacking the little girl. Be careful! We don't want to harm the baby, but when you have a clear chance, shoot him!"

Rebecca's mother could see what was really happening. "STOP!" she screamed at the policemen. "He's trying to *save* my baby!"

Just then little Rebecca wriggled out of Murphy's grip and fell into the deep water at the end of the dock. Before anyone could reach the end of the dock to save her, Murphy jumped in and gently lifted her to the surface by the back of her shirt.

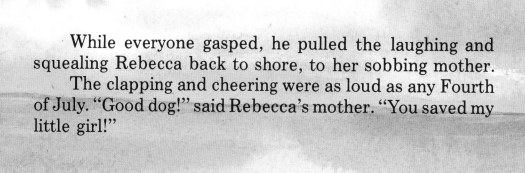

While everyone gasped, he pulled the laughing and squealing Rebecca back to shore, to her sobbing mother. The clapping and cheering were as loud as any Fourth of July. "Good dog!" said Rebecca's mother. "You saved my little girl!"

Ludgie Brown was the first to speak up. "Why, this isn't a mad dog! He and I were just sharing my root beer back at the grocery store."

"Yes! He's a great dog," added old Mr. Johnson. He comes by my barber shop almost every morning, and I offer him doughnuts."

"He can have the biggest bones from my butcher shop!" put in Mr. Sneed.

Sheriff Forbus blew his whistle to quiet the crowd. He cleared his throat. "This dog is a hero!" he said. "He saved little Rebecca's life. Who does he belong to?"

No one knew, because Murphy the Mutt was nobody's dog.

"Then I hereby declare this dog our Official Town Dog," pronounced Sheriff Forbus.

"Hooray!" shouted all the boys and girls who played in the park.

"Wonderful!" added the shoppers and Mr. Sneed, the grocer.

"Goo gog!" cooed little Rebecca, hugging the wet dog. Clem Loggins, the newspaper editor, took their picture. "Now I've got some news!" he muttered to himself as he hurried off.

Everyone in town offered to adopt Murphy, but Sheriff Forbus invited him to sleep at the police station. "A special dog needs a special place," the sheriff explained with a smile. Warm, gentle breezes lulled Murphy into a welcome nap. For the first time, he had his own place to lay his head.

The next day there was a picture of Murphy on the front page of the *Taylorsville Chit-Chat*. He was receiving a huge medal from the mayor.

Now everywhere Murphy goes, people call out to him cheerfully. They offer him food and stroke his soft brown fur. No one knows who named him Murphy, but he's a hero to everyone in Taylorsville. And best of all, Murphy the Hero is everybody's dog.